aura
alphabet

32900

THE HANDMADE ALPHABET

Laura Rankin

DIAL BOOKS NEW YORK

For Nick and Brendan, with love

The artist and publisher appreciate the help of
Alan Barwiolek, M.A.,
American Sign Language/Deaf Culture Consultant.

Published by Dial Books
A Division of Penguin Books USA Inc.
375 Hudson Street
New York, New York 10014

Design by Nancy R. Leo
Printed in Hong Kong
by South China Printing Company (1988) Limited

3 5 7 9 10 8 6 4 2

Library of Congress Cataloging in Publication Data
Rankin, Laura.
The handmade alphabet / by Laura Rankin.
p.   cm.
Summary: Presents the manual alphabet,
used in American Sign Language.
ISBN 0-8037-0974-9 (trade). — ISBN 0-8037-0975-7 (library)
1. Deaf — Means of communication. [1. Alphabet. 2. Deaf.]
I. Title.
HV2480.R36 1991   419 — dc20   [E]   90-24593   CIP   AC

The art for each picture consists of colored pencil on charcoal paper,
which is scanner-separated and reproduced in full color.

Artist's Note

My older stepson is deaf. For the first eighteen years of his life he moved with dignity yet difficulty through the hearing world, relying primarily on the complex art of lipreading for his verbal understanding. Then he went to Gallaudet University in Washington, D.C., and learned American Sign Language. As a visual language it was completely accessible to him and allowed him to share ideas fully. Through it he gained more thorough understanding and total communication.

The manual alphabet, an integral part of American Sign Language, was my first contact with signing. As an outsider to deaf culture, my abilities in this mode are limited. However, my respect is deep and it is my wish that this introduction to the alphabet begin to open the world of sign communication to all who see this book.

—LAURA RANKIN
Buffalo, New York

A

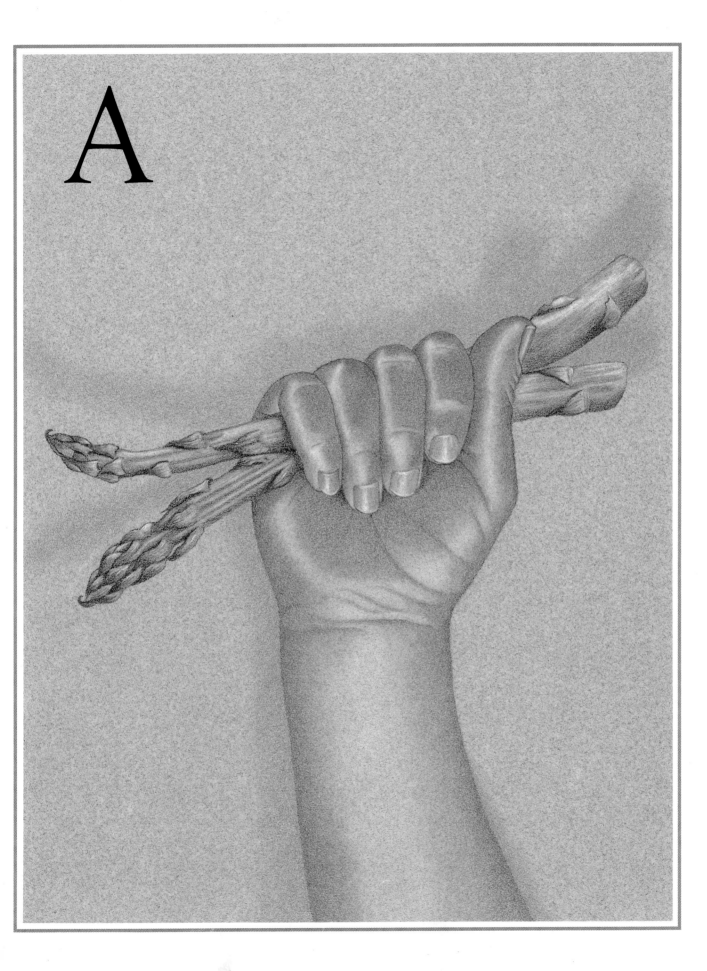

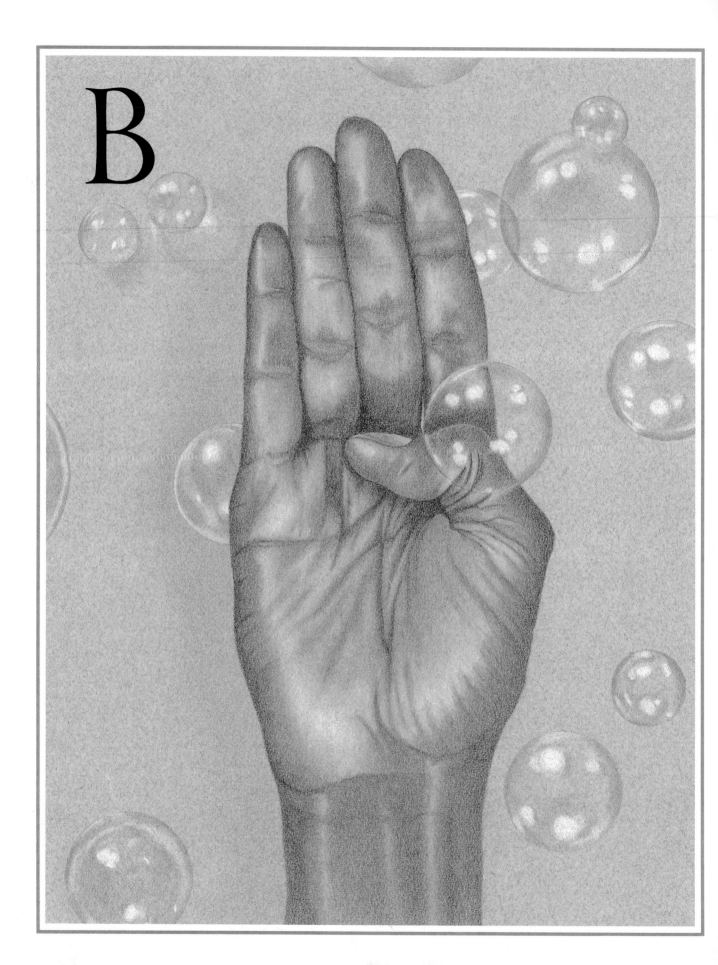

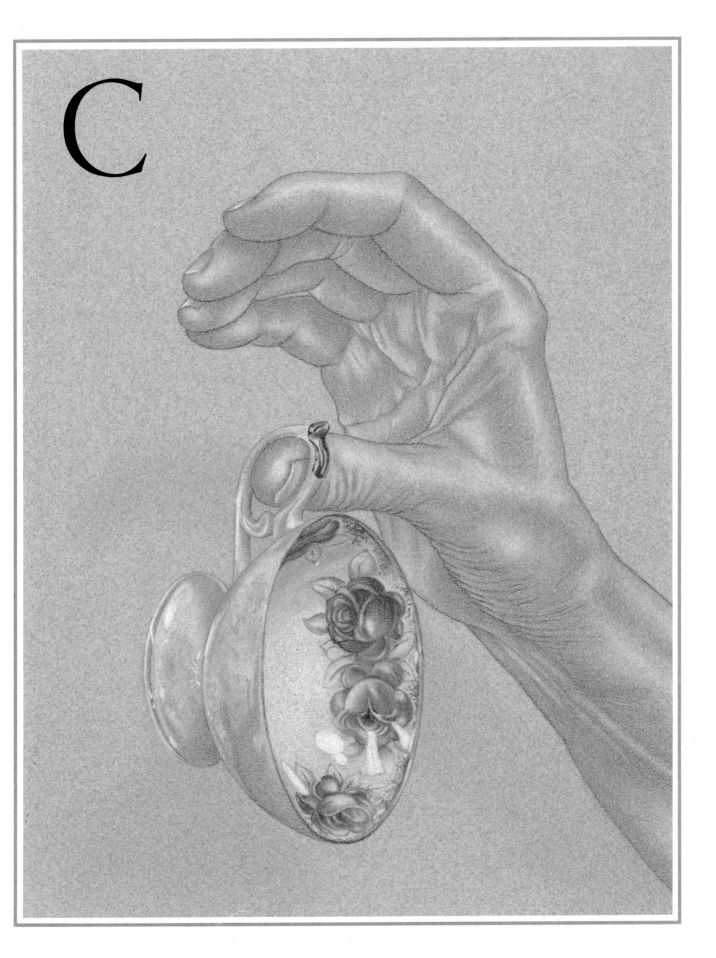

E

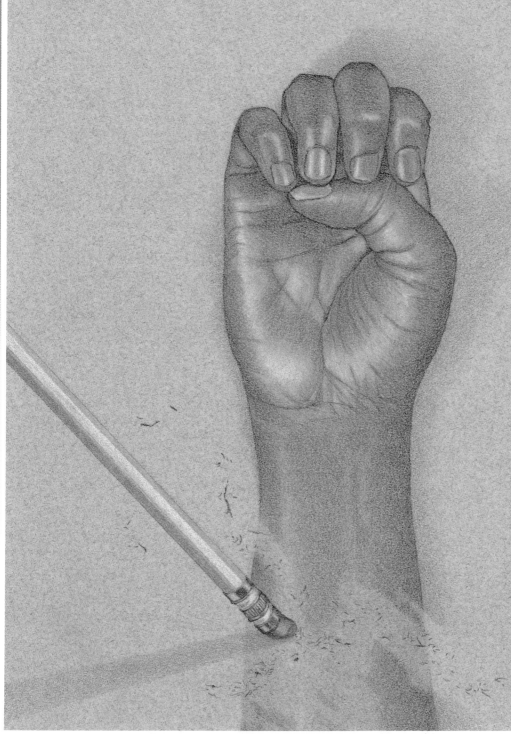

F

G

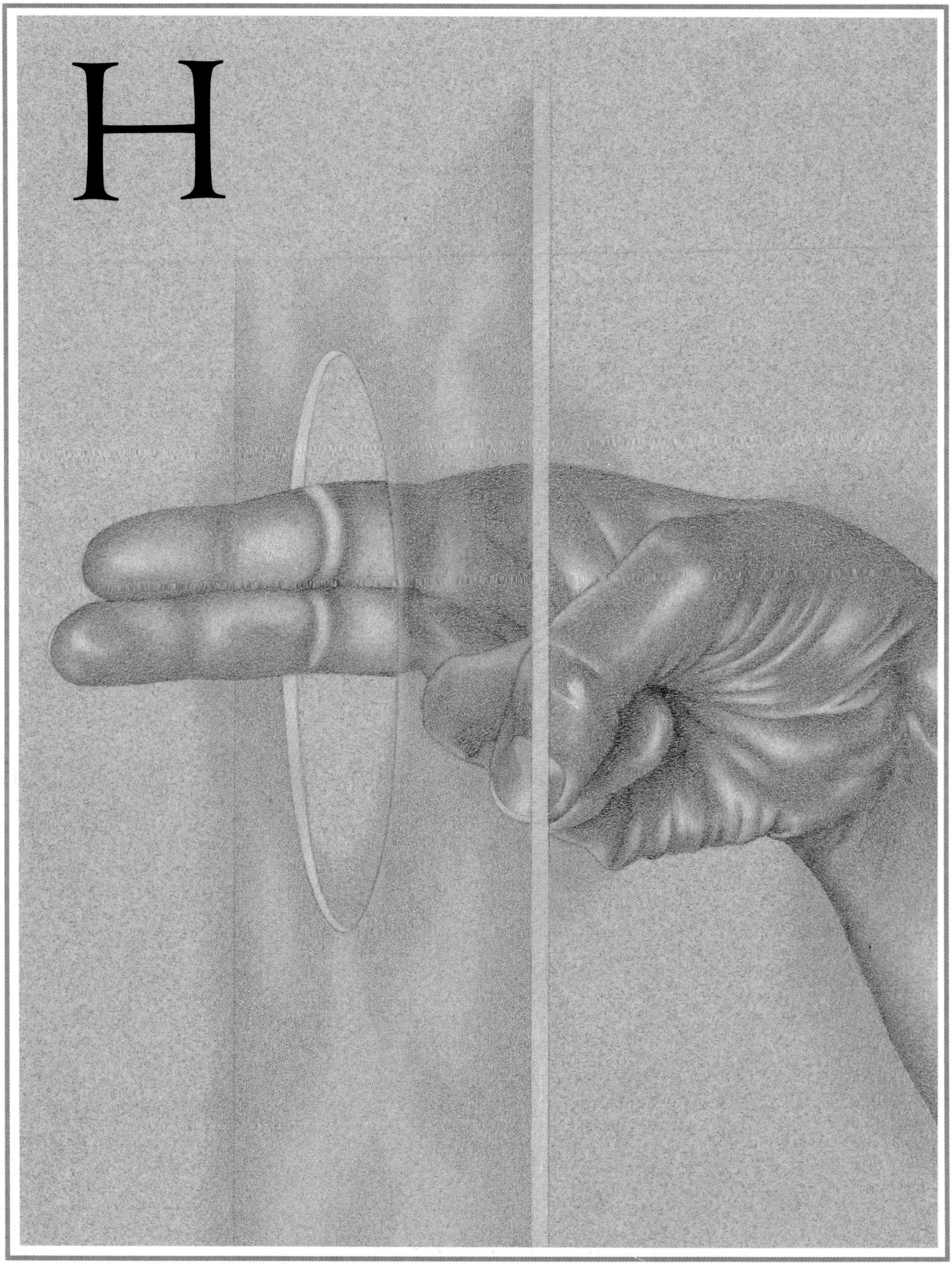
H

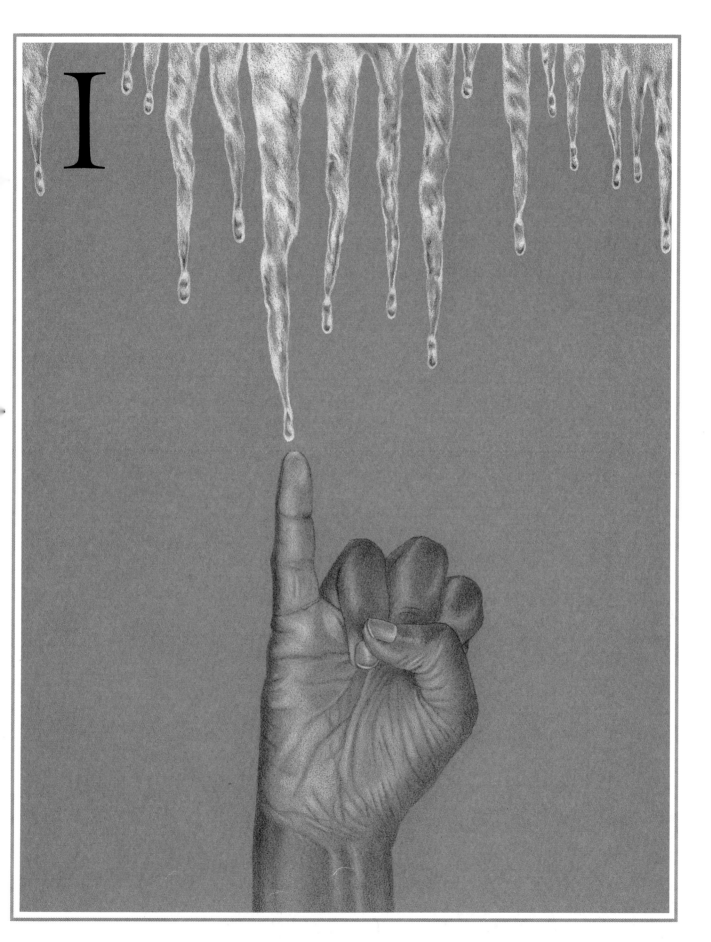

I

J

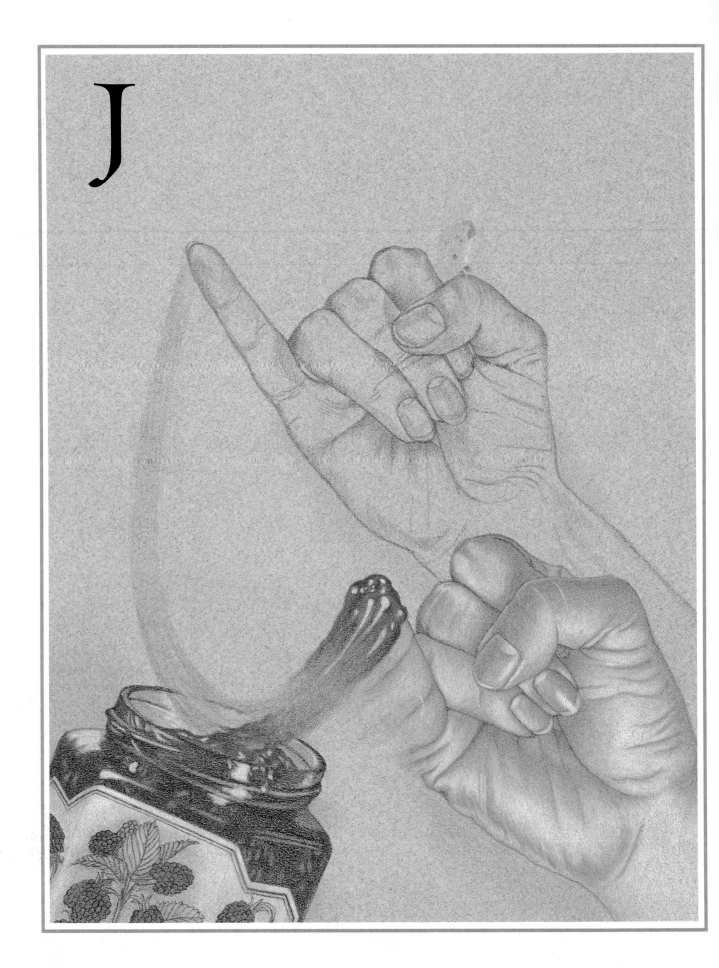

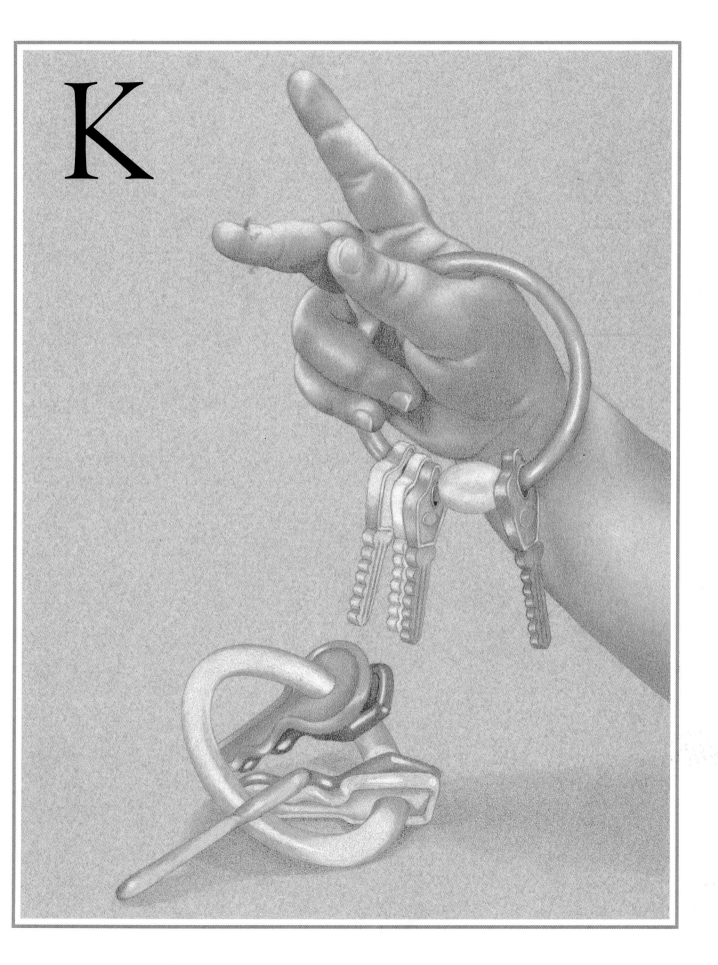

L

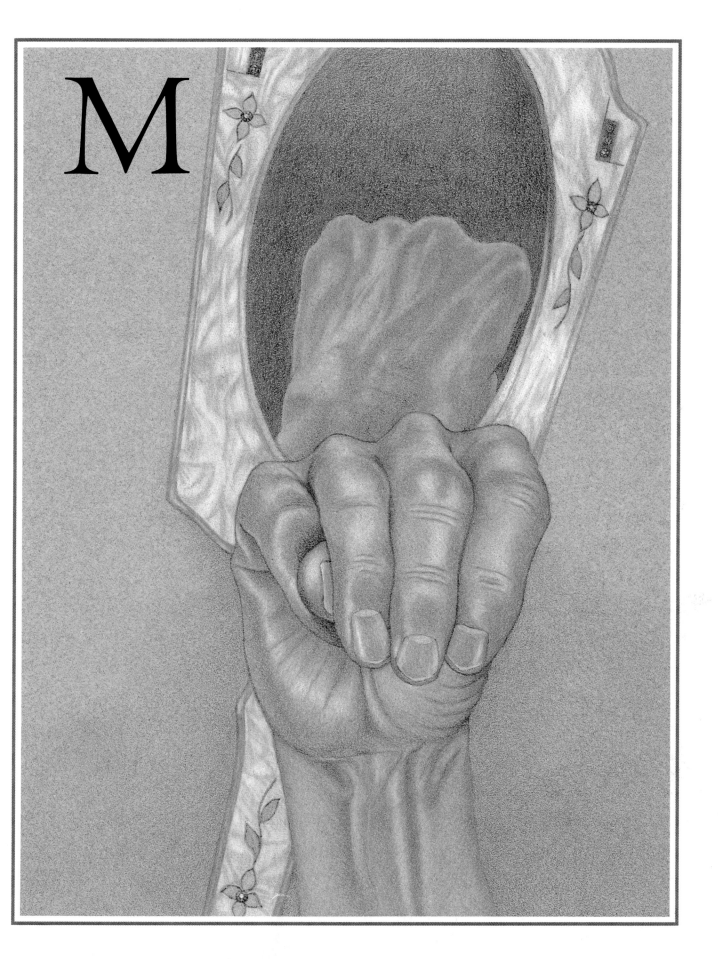

M

N

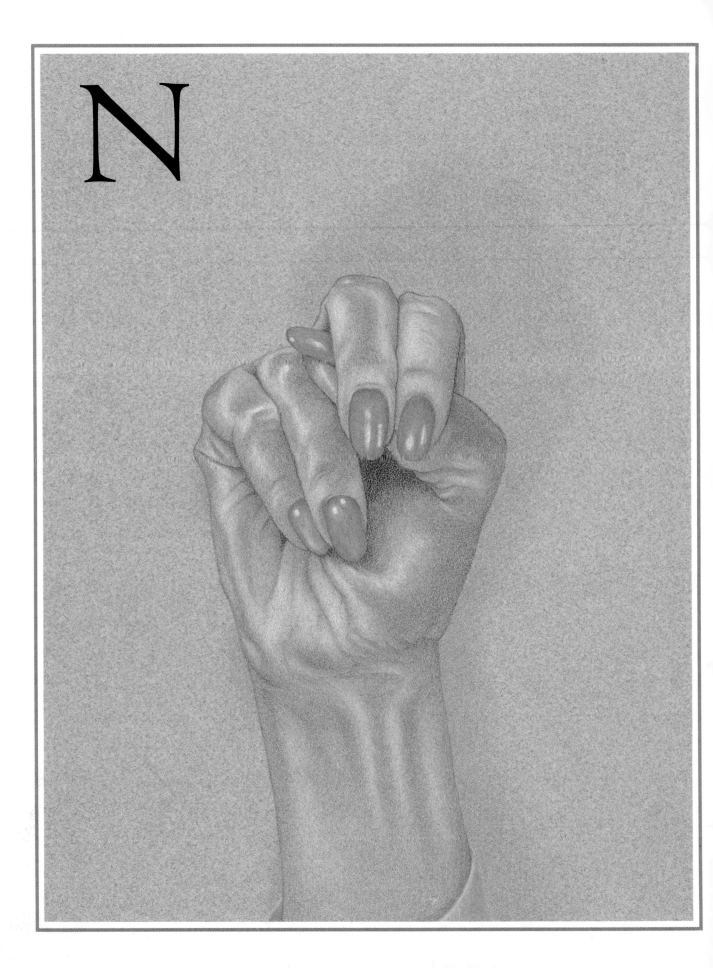

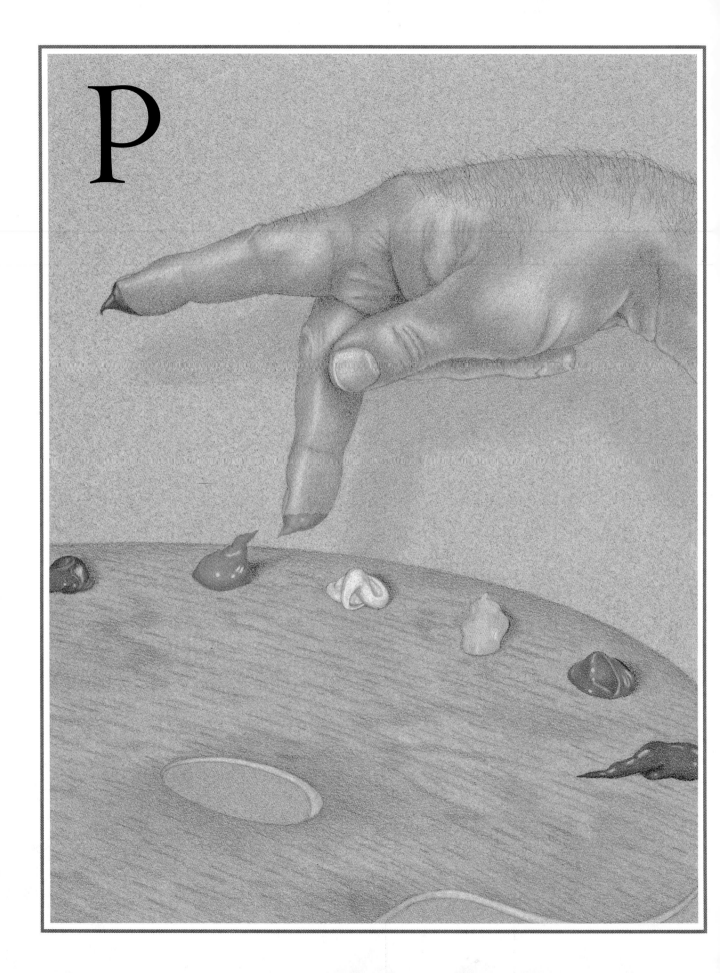

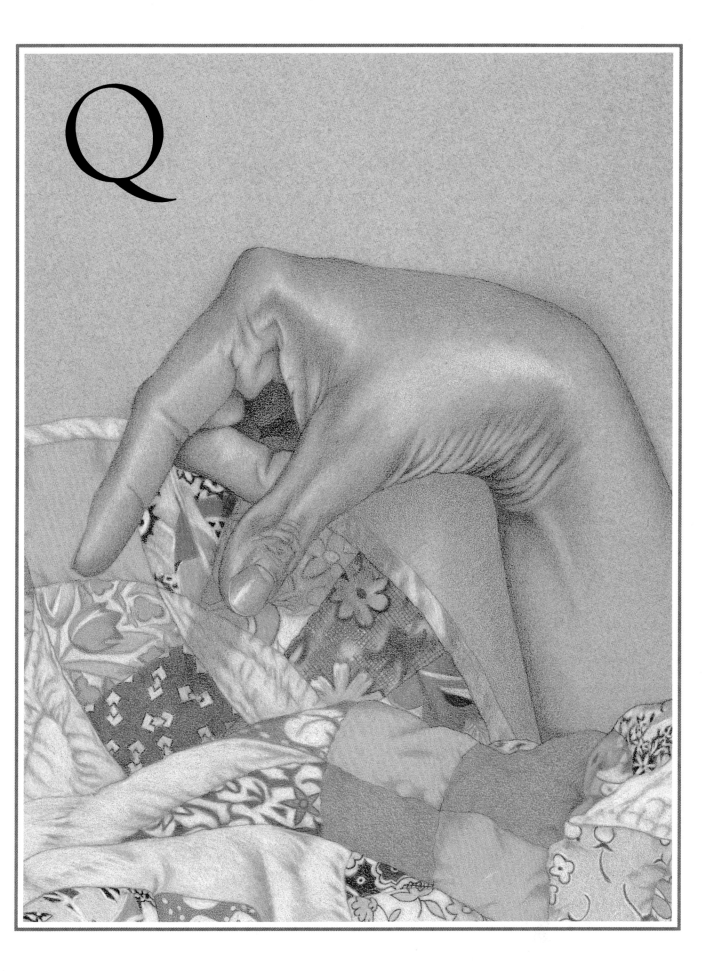